River of No Return

by Julia Hanna
illustrated by Will Williams

 HOUGHTON MIFFLIN   BOSTON

White Water Country

The car squeaked as it jolted over the bumpy road. Linzee sniffed the sharp, sweet smell of the pine trees and squinted at the deep blue Idaho sky. On the airplane from Seattle to Boise, her mom had told her about the Salmon River. They would spend the week white-water rafting. Linzee's mother said that people came to test themselves against the river's rapids.

Mom is always testing things, Linzee thought. The car bounced. Linzee's stomach jumped.

"Listen!" Mom said. Linzee heard a roar. It sounded like a huge train. Mom pointed at a green strip of water snaking through the pines below: "There's the Salmon!"

Linzee could see how fast the river was moving. The flashes of white water winked at her in the sun. It was as if the river knew she was afraid. *But Mom's smile only gets bigger the closer we get to the river*, Linzee thought. Mom had been planning this vacation for a long time.

The car stopped in a clearing near the river. Guides put water containers in three rubber rafts and gathered rope into loops. They talked about a bear they'd seen fishing in the river. The guides wore matching baseball caps that said RIVER OF NO RETURN in big letters across the top. *They're just trying to scare us*, Linzee thought. *This river can't be that bad — or can it?*

"Hey, Lin, give me your duffel bag," Mom said.

Linzee handed it over without saying anything. The last time Mom had rafted the Salmon, Linzee had been four years old and had stayed at home with her grandmother.

Mom had shown Linzee photos of the trip. Her dad was in those pictures — it was right before he died. *We're here because of Dad,* Linzee thought. *He and Mom went on trips like these all the time. They learned how to take a raft through white water together. Now Mom wants to show me the same thing.* But Linzee's stomach felt heavy when she imagined herself rafting in the churning white water.

A guide named Dave handed out life jackets and helmets. "We're starting on an easy part today. But make sure you buckle up anyway." He smiled at Linzee. She felt some of the weight in her stomach melt away.

"How easy?" she asked.

"Small waves, clear passages, and plenty of sandbanks to rest on along the way," he said. "We'll go slow in the beginning — don't worry."

"This is her first trip," said Mom. "Linzee and I hope to take on some of the real rapids by the end of our stay."

Linzee's stomach churned when Mom talked about the rapids. But it was time to go now — the rafts were packed.

Linzee stepped into their raft and sat down. She could feel the river running beneath the raft's rubber bottom. The others climbed aboard, and then the raft glided into the current. *We're not attached to anything*, Linzee thought. *It feels good to float free.* She shut her eyes. The river smelled musty, as if it came from deep inside the earth.

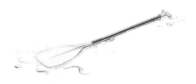

Not So Bad

"Asleep already?" Dave joked. He handed Linzee a paddle. Three people sat on each side, and Dave showed them how to paddle with a smooth, easy motion.

"Don't fight the river," he warned. "You'll never win. Think ahead, watch out for obstacles, and you'll be okay." The raft bounced up and down a little.

"Those are riffles," said Mom. "When the water runs over rocks on the bottom of the river, it makes riffles." Linzee took a few strokes with the paddle. It wasn't so hard after all.

As they moved downstream, Dave taught them how to turn the boat. To go right, the command was, "Right side back paddle, left side forward paddle." *Wouldn't you have to move the right side paddle forward to turn right?* Linzee wondered. But when she paddled backward, she understood how it worked. You could turn the raft by pushing against the river. You were using the river's power to turn a big raft.

"There's a clearing around this bend," Dave said. "We'll take the raft out there."

That night, Mom asked, "How was your first day?"

"Not so bad," Linzee said. "I just don't know if I'm ready for the rough water yet."

"Well, you did great," Mom said. "Tomorrow, we'll see a little choppier water, but we'll take it slow."

After dinner, people told stories around the campfire. One woman told how her husband had been flipped overboard when they hit a wave. "I tried to paddle back," she said, "but the current was too strong. His life jacket saved him."

"Never go back if someone falls out," Dave said. "It won't help. You need to focus ahead. The river won't wait."

When Linzee went to bed, she lay awake for a while thinking about the stories. *The river won't wait,* kept running through her mind.

The River Won't Wait

Linzee woke the next morning with a start. She had been in the middle of a bad dream. In the dream, someone had fallen out of a raft that she was in.

After breakfast, Linzee stood on the bank and watched the water rush past. *The river won't wait*, she said to herself.

Today they would be rafting down a different part of the river. There would be some waves. It would be choppier than yesterday. Dave said there would be rocks too.

Out on the river, Linzee did her best to keep up with the paddling. She watched the water rushing underneath. Mom calmly moved her paddle from side to side like an expert.

Linzee didn't find this part of the river easy. Yesterday it had been wide and flat, with meadows and wildflowers lining the banks. Here, sharp gray ledges rose on both sides.

"You're doing great," Mom said. "In a couple of days you'll be a pro."

How do you know? Linzee wondered. *How do you know I won't make a mistake and get smashed against the rocks?*

"Right side back paddle, left side forward paddle!" Dave shouted.

Their raft bumped around a boulder and scooted forward. Linzee fought to keep her paddle in the water.

"Go with it!" Mom shouted through a huge smile.

She hasn't been this happy in a while, Linzee thought. *Okay, go with it. Focus on what's ahead, just like Dave says.*

The raft hopped down a little waterfall. Thoomp! *Rubber bounces*, Linzee thought. *Rubber rafts bounce.* The waves didn't seem so big anymore. Then Dave said it was time to break for lunch.

"Already?" Linzee asked. "It was just getting fun!"

Dave laughed. "You're turning into a real river rat."

A man in a canoe brought a two-person raft to camp that night. It was small, with long oars instead of paddles. Right away Mom signed up to take it out the next day with Linzee.

I just got used to the big raft, Linzee thought.

"Don't worry, I'll row," Mom said. "We might even try some rapids, since you're such a pro now. It'll be more fun than a roller coaster."

Linzee nodded. *Yeah, right, a roller coaster*, she thought. She wasn't so sure about the real white water. But Mom seemed so sure she was ready. *I guess I am.*

That night, Linzee could hear the river muttering to itself.

No Return!

The next morning, Linzee and her mom tied their duffel bags into the two-person raft and pushed off into the current. Linzee waved to Dave and the others as they disappeared around a bend. The water rushed and foamed against the rocks. The river wasn't muttering anymore. It was shouting and pounding like an angry giant. Then Linzee saw a dead tree trunk up ahead.

"Turn, Mom! Turn!" she shouted.

"Which way?" Mom yelled. "You have to tell me which way!"

Too late. The raft banged hard against the tree.

Mom stood and leaned against the oars.

We could get pinned here, Linzee thought. *Trapped against the tree for as long as the river wants to keep us.*

But they broke free and raced on. Linzee saw big waves ahead. She shut her eyes and gripped the slippery raft. Then there was a splash.

"Mom!" she screamed. She saw the flash of Mom's orange life jacket swirling in the dark water. The oars flopped loosely against the raft.

17

A wave slapped the raft sideways. Icy water washed over Linzee. *Get those oars*, Linzee thought. *The river won't wait.* She grabbed the oars, gasped for breath, and pulled.

The raft tilted and plunged forward, then backward, then forward again.

Linzee could see a dip in the water spinning like a whirlpool. Rafters called these spots "holes." Holes were almost impossible to get out of if you were all alone. She screamed.

The end of an oar pushed her hand up and hit her chin, hard. The river blurred. A bubble of pain burst in her head. *Pull hard*, was all she thought.

Linzee pulled. The river yanked back with invisible hands. She pulled again, and again, until her back and arms burned. Water hammered the raft from all sides.

I can't stay here, she thought. *I can't.*

Linzee threw her weight against the oars. The raft moved up and over the hole's edge. *I'm out! Stay straight. Lean back over the dip. Pull right around the boulder.* The oars twisted in her hands. Her mind raced faster than the river. As the raft spun around, she saw an orange speck in the dark river behind her.

The raft lurched sideways, then turned again. It was backwards. *Don't panic. Think*, she told herself.

The raft spun around. Linzee's hands hurt. Linzee shut her eyes and pulled the paddle as hard as she could one last time. The raft twirled, then jolted downstream.

Seconds later, the river was quiet. *I made it*, Linzee thought, *I made it through white water. But Mom! Where is Mom?*

The oars felt like huge logs in her hands. Linzee took a deep breath. *Get to shore. If you run back along the river, you might find her*, she thought.

But something plunged inside Linzee's stomach. *What if I don't find her?*

The words on Dave's cap flashed in her mind: *RIVER OF NO RETURN.*

The river didn't care that she only had Mom.

Just then something big and orange slapped against the side of the raft. The thud knocked Linzee onto her back. Then she saw a wet hand coming over the edge.

"Mom!" she cried, jumping up to help her soaked mother crawl back into the raft.

With a laugh that could be heard all the way back to camp, Mom grabbed Linzee in a great big bear hug. "You made it! Linzee! You made it! You did it alone!"

Linzee hugged her mother and started laughing too.

Maybe the Salmon was called the River of No Return, but someday she and Mom would come back to raft the white water.

And Linzee would be ready for it.